THE HOUSE ON THE DUNES

ROBERTO VIOLA

Translated by Yolanda De Mola, S.C.

PAULIST PRESS
New York/Mahwah, NJ

Cover illustration by Kathleen Fiske. Cover design by Moe Berman.

Originally published in Spanish as *La Casilla de las Dunas,* copyright
© 1981 by Roberto Viola. English translation copyright © 1993 by
Roberto Viola.

Library of Congress Cataloging-in Publication Data

Viola, Roberto, 1927-
    [Casilla de las dunas. English]
    The house on the dunes/Roberto Viola; translated by Yolanda
De Mola.
        p. cm.
    ISBN 0-8091-3419-5 (ptk.)
    I. Title.
PQ8520.32.I65C3713   1993   93-23066
863—dc20   CIP

Published by Paulist Press
997 Macarthur Blvd.
Mahwah, N.J. 07430

They set out very early one morning to go fishing under a clear sky and with a north wind.

They returned at nightfall. Then they had supper.

On the following morning the north wind was again blowing.

Twenty-four hours. A single spin of the earth on its axis. In those 24 hours there took place a filtering of memories that belong to the past and to times that go beyond the calendar, extraordinary, mysterious: some of them imaginary and others as real as the blood that courses through one's veins.

As if the 24 hours were spattered with the foam of eternity.

Fishing

1.

They were walking down a road along the dunes.

Two travelers. Walking.

They carried two fishing rods, two old hats and a knapsack.

The newly risen sun hid behind some storm clouds that danced in the sky.

"Are we going fishing today?"

"Of course, boy. Today is our day. Get that into your head." The old man tapped on Juan's head with the bony knuckles of his hand.

"Oh? And what are we going to fish, don Andrés?"

"Sargos."

"Will we fill the knapsack?"

"Yes."

Juan began to run around the old man. He could see in his mind's eye the silvery fish jumping between the stones of the shoals.

"How do you know we'll catch fish today, don Andrés?"

The old man began to whistle a tune that Juan did not recognize. The gentle north wind ruffled the boy's unfastened shirt causing it to flutter like a flag. The old man, with one hand pressed down on his hat that covered part of his large ears.

"How do you know, don Andrés, that we're going to catch fish today?"

"That's my secret."

"Tell it to me."

"You already know it, but you don't know that you do."

The old man resumed his rapid pace.

"You told me, don Andrés, that you'd teach me to fish."

"Of course. Fishing is the most difficult science in the world."

"More difficult than going to the moon?"

"Much more," he answered teasingly. "Anyone can go to the moon. But only the one who understands life can learn to fish."

Juan shrugged his shoulders. The old man had some strange notions.

The sky was clearing. The fresh north wind and the first oblique rays of the sun produced in him a beautiful sensation of well-being that ran through his body.

"I wish summer would last all year long," he exclaimed.

"That would not be good."

"Why wouldn't it be good?"

The old man began to whistle again. This time it sounded like a small toy flute.

"Do you know how old I am? Thirteen..."

"Just one year ago today you came to this little house," commented the old man.

Juan had lost all sense of time. At times it seemed to him that he had always lived by the sea.

"Only a year?" he asked.

"A year is a long time."

6

"It seems to me that I've always lived in this place."

They cut through the sandbank, walking slowly. Each step caused them an added effort. Their feet sank in the sand up to their ankles. They rose and fell continually. In the dunes there are zones of quicksand. Anyone off his guard who steps into those sections sinks and dies, buried and without leaving a trace.

"Am I now a disciple of the sea?"

"Do you want to be?"

"It's what I want most in life," answered Juan with conviction.

"I think so. I think you are about to become a disciple."

Juan ran down the hill. He sank his short legs in the sand up to his knees. Thus did he arrive at the seashore ahead of the old man.

It was eight o'clock in the morning.

2.

The cork floated in rhythm with the waves in a continuous rise and fall. The noonday sun was reflected on the water in a variety of colors.

"See the rays across the water!" he whispered. A dark red band along the breakers. The old man explained that the band was not dark red but pearl gray. Juan did not understand. In the distance the sea was covered by a milky fringe and another that was green, a deep green that extended to the horizon.

7

The green sea was his favorite and the favorite of the fish too.

One night, speaking about colors, the old man informed him about the existence of black waters, as black as ink.

"But is the sea black?" he asked.

"The sea is never black."

Juan heaved a sigh of relief and abandoned the thought of black waters. From time to time, a huge wave that seemed to rise from the bottom of the ocean would crash against the rocks and splash the fishermen.

The old man looked as solid as the rock by the breakers. From the shape of his lips, Juan realized he was humming a song. At times, when they were fishing side by side, he would hear something. At other times no matter how much he tried to listen, he heard not a sound. When he was able to hear the song, he felt a tingling sensation pass through his body, the same feeling that the north wind produced in him early in the morning.

Perhaps the old man was calling the fish with his music. That was a question he must ask him that night before they went to bed:

"Tell me, don Andrés, does your song attract the fish?"

Some day he would learn to hum. For now he found it impossible. Juan squirmed on his seat of stone. He was hungry and had a great desire to speak. He had remained still for four hours, without a complaint, without a question or a comment. The old man would not have liked to see him weak and talkative.

3.

One day, after a long time, bored of waiting so long and furious at the immobility and silence of don Andrés, Juan began to scream and to throw stones into the water. His target was the old man's bluish buoy. The old man, without turning his head, gathered his fishing rod and left. At sunset, Juan, sick at heart, walked toward the little house. He became lost in the dunes until, exhausted, he fell asleep on the deserted beach.

The next day the radiant sun awakened him. He looked for the shack all morning and all afternoon. He asked for don Andrés of the few fishermen he met along the way; but no one could give him news of the old man.

Finally, on the third day, feverish and with sores on his feet, he saw the shack on the sandy desert. Desperate, he ran the final stretch. There sat the old man, at the door.

"Don Andrés?" he shouted.

The old man stroked his head, made him sit in his place and served him half of a white sea bass with a piece of home-made bread and a glass of wine. Juan felt blissfully happy. So happy that his feet stopped hurting as if by magic.

4.

It was complete solitude. During the course of the morning a pair of fishermen passed by. For a while they cast their fishing lines into the serene waters. From the corner of their eyes they observed their empty knapsack. After a while, they departed without a word.

He felt pity. The old man had been so sure of finding sargos. Perhaps he's too old, he thought. He's confusing dreams with reality.

Could the old man ever have been his age? He could not imagine him young. Nor did he like the idea.

How many were the wrinkles around his small and shining eyes? No one could count them. Must he not be tired? Perhaps he was hungry. Could he be annoyed at the fishes he was calling so uselessly?

Perhaps the fish were sleeping or just not hungry...Perhaps their bait was suspended in a void under the sea and they might wait year after year. He would grow old like the old man and the old man would die many times over....

How stupid! One can die only once. Die only once, be born only once, and get old only once. But fishing can be done many times, yesterday, today, tomorrow, next year...

Perhaps the old man is fishing for the last time. Always when they went fishing it seemed to him that don Andrés was doing it for the last time.

A wave not strong enough to lash against the rock licked his feet. The float raised its reddish head. Juan immediately gathered his thoughts and concentrated on the line.

The float settled back on the water whitened by the sun. The old man raised his fishing rod. He held it between his knees while he changed the bait. He cleaned the fishing hook assiduously until it shone.

From his pocket he pulled out a sardine which he placed on a wooden splint. He cut a piece he felt was just right. He pierced the meat with the hook covering the sharp pointed steel completely. He cleaned the knife. He wrapped the fish inside a newspaper, rinsed the piece of wood in water caught in the cleft of the rock, and once again the float rested on the waters some three meters from the coast.

Juan liked to go out fishing with the old man. And he liked the night before when they would prepare the fishing rods, sharpen the fish hooks, knot the fishing line, observe the weather, predict the arrival of clear waters, note the tides, distinguish cloud from cloud and note their significance: the small reed-like ones on the horizon so often traitorous...

"What is there after death, don Andrés?"

He mustn't forget to ask him that question. Ghosts are the dead who return to frighten the living. Juan did not believe in them, but he was not encouraged by saying he did not believe in them, fearful he would provoke them to appear during the night.

"What happens to a fish after it dies?"

If a man eats the fish, the latter becomes the man. Juan's thoughts made him nervous because they often became as tangled as the lines of his tackle.

You have to find the tip and little by little, with gentle fingers, begin passing the thread this way and that. The task could take hours and demands the same patience as fishing.

He felt like throwing himself in the water and laughing as long as the sun was out.

"Where are the sargos and the eels, don Andrés? You promised me some, didn't you?"

This was a bad thought. The kind of thought that scares away the fish.

5.

The old man explained to him the importance of thoughts in the art of fishing. He taught him how to distinguish between the bad ones and the good. Formerly, he entertained whatever thoughts might pass through his head; now he had them well under control, because catching fish depended on one's thoughts. The fisherman is a beggar of the sea. This is a good thought.

"Why is it good, don Andrés?"

"Because it is true."

"Did you ever ask for alms?"

"Of course, we're both beggars. All people are beggars."

"And the rich?"

"They too."

"My uncle would be furious if you told him he was a beggar."

"Your uncle is blind. Many men are blind."

Juan did not understand. Nor did he care whether or not he understood with his head. Now he knew he was a beggar. The old man and he were beggars of the sea. This thought filled him with joy: beggar and disciple.

"Does the sea have many disciples?"

"Many."

"I don't see them."

"You meet them now and then. Those meetings

are special days. Once, for example, many years ago, I met a disciple of the sea; we lived and fished together. Romualdo loved the fish, he respected them, thought about them, called to them and would not be annoyed if they did not come to him.

"When no one else was catching anything, we would return with our knapsacks filled with cod, flounder, eels and more."

"Other fishermen would visit us at night to question us: Where had we gone, what bait did we use, what kind of hook... The following day our fisherman had become famous and many people came to him with their fishing rods, with poles of every size and condition..."

"We would migrate elsewhere and the fish would follow us because we were friends. Thoughts are more important than bait."

Yes, perhaps he did not have the right thoughts and that is why the float of his line remained inactive amid the waves.

6.

"What happened to Romualdo, don Andrés?"

The old man stirred the coals in the fireplace, rekindling a dying ember. Then a south wind shook the tiny house. The sand slipped through the hinges. Juan wrapped himself in a blanket. On stormy nights the old man spoke; the sun seemed to silence him.

"Have I ever told you about Romualdo, boy?"

Unlike other people, the old man never repeated his stories, perhaps because he spoke little.

"No."

"Romualdo was lame, he used to drag his left leg. His footprints in the sand had a curious shape. He and I built this shack with wood we found along the coast after a storm."

"Where did he sleep before that?"

"Before I came, Romualdo slept outdoors in a small pine forest. He knew the sea, the fishermen, the fish, the bait, the birds that inhabit the coastline, the insects, the crabs...."

"He knew how to control the dunes and change their movement."

"One morning a jeep arrived. Two men and a young woman got off it. The woman called: 'Papa, papa!' The men lifted him up in the air, put him in the jeep and took him away."

After a moment of silence, he continued:

"They put him in an asylum for old people who cannot care for themselves."

"Why didn't they leave him with you by the sea?"

"They had been searching for him for a year. His name appeared in the newspapers."

"Why didn't they leave him in peace, don Andrés?"

He remembered that night well. Although there was little light in the shack, he was sure he saw a great sadness come over the face of the old man. Perhaps he didn't see the sorrow, but felt it throughout his body.

The old man cleared his throat.

"Romualdo was a disciple of the sea. A good disciple, and the sea has enemies."

"Why does the sea have enemies?"

14

"They locked him up," he continued, "in a small room painted in white with a bed that was also white. Romualdo shouted that they free him. Free him to return to the coast. They locked the door and he continued to shout so they gave him a sedative. Romualdo felt his strength ebbing away and threw himself on the floor. Two nurses came and gently put him in the white bed. When he woke up, he refused to take anything. They gave him an injection. He went back to sleep and in three days he was dead."

Juan felt a sudden chill. Romualdo must have been a great man and the enemy killed him. Besides the chill, he felt anger, the same sort of rage he felt at a football game when the decision was made that favored the opposing team.

"Why didn't the sea defend Romualdo?"

With the strength it has, thought Juan, it could have ground his enemies to powder.

"How do you know it did not defend him?" asked the old man. "The sea never abandons its friends."

His rage left his mouth little by little; but his head could not comprehend how the sea helped if it let its friends die.

The water began to boil in the kettle.

7.

At four in the afternoon the red float of the line began to fall open: First there appeared a rose halo through which one could see the blue water; later

15

the halo seemed to assume its own personality and was transformed into another buoy, a Siamese sister of the first.

Juan closed and opened his eyes trying to dispel the illusion. He had spent eight hours waiting, without moving, without speaking, without eating, under the sun's rays. Some boats had sailed away beyond the horizon. The wind had circled from north to east: It was the sea breeze.

Had the old man lived with or been transformed into a rock? Had he had a wife? Children? They had lived together for a year. He had never questioned him about his former life. Several times he had been tempted to do so but he had always stopped himself. That night when they were returning home, he would say to him:

"Have you ever been married, don Andrés?" or

"Do you have any children, don Andrés?" or

"Have you always lived in the dunes?"

No! He would not ask about his family. Instead, he would ask him about his enemies and his friends.

Since the old man told him the story of Romualdo, Juan was afraid that a jeep might appear amid the dunes. Romualdo's own daughter had been his enemy. How strange! Perhaps the old man had no children; perhaps no one knew him.

8.

"If I am a disciple of the sea," he asked, "shall I have enemies too?"

"Of course, the sea's enemies will be your enemies."

"Who are the sea's enemies, don Andrés?"

"Don't worry about knowing your enemies, boy; get to know your friends."

A small marine crab was moving its long claws lazily. At first, before the old man did anything, Juan felt fear and disgust. He confused a large spider crab for a tarantula.

"No," explained don Andrés, gathering it up gently between his fingers. Marine crabs travel many kilometers on the sea on the back of the raging waters. Thereafter he befriended those crabs and no longer mixed them up with spider crabs he had seen on his uncle's property.

"You know, boy, the crabs are the ones that transport anemones, those tiny flowers that settle on the rocks."

From the time that the old man showed him those maritime transporters, Juan also became a friend of the water currents. How many fish are there in the sea? How many stars in the sky? The fishes are the stars of the sea.

The old man explained to him that there are fish that have very strange forms and marvelous colors.

"Imagine the strangest shape."

"What do you mean?"

"I want you to imagine the strangest shape you could possibly imagine. A crab here, another there, a flat head, two eyes on one side, a mouth way over there...."

Juan made a design on the sand while seated on a trunk by the shack.

"I assure you," said the old man, "that a fish like that exists somewhere in some other part of the sea."

"Have you seen all kinds of fishes, don Andrés?"

"No, boy."

After that day, Juan continued shaping fish of the rarest forms in the sand. That way he became familiar with the inhabitants of the ocean.

"Why are men not fish?" That was another question he would ask the old man. Why is it that with as many fish in the sea as there are stars in the sky that none of them bit his fish hook and sank the float of his line out of sight to the bottom of the sea?

"Tell me, don Andrés, are there more fish than men, women and children?"

"Many more."

"Are the inhabitants of the sea more numerous than the inhabitants on land?"

"Yes."

How strange! One looks at the earth and sees people, birds, animals, a cat, a dog, sheep, worms...One looks at the sea and sees a desert...

Of course fishermen recognize in the movement of the waters the presence of schools of fishes. There are dolphins also riding the waves and showing off their black and robust bodies.

"What do dolphins do?"

"They're cowboys of the deep; they gather together flocks of fishes."

The inhabitants of the land cannot enter into the interior of the sea. And the dwellers of the sea cannot invade the land; each has its own domain. The fisherman is an invader seated on the frontier between two empires.

18

9.

Juan began to imagine an invasion from the sea: enormous waves like the promontory, tall as a skyscraper. At first it's a moving hill like soft pendants seen on the horizon, that approach slowly and, upon reaching the shore, curve their backs like an angry cat with its hair on end, becoming claws with nails of foam, and crash against the reefs.

Covered by the water, Juan is tossed about like the little float from his fishing line, lifted, pushed, gasping for breath, almost drowning.

"The sea is invading the land," he shouts. "The fishes are getting even with us."

The air returns to his lungs. He feels comfortable, light-headed. The old man grabs his arm.

"Come," he says. "I'm going to show you the sea and all its fishes. You'll see each of the ones you drew on the sand by the shack."

The light is diffused and brilliant. The sea is calm within. As bad as it might appear when viewed from without, but as good as when one is a dweller on it. He saw sargos of all sizes.

"Don Andrés! Don Andrés! A school of sargos!"

There were also some conger eels which in the sea looked like small, white sepias. He felt a tingling through his body. They were displacing a host of mackerel, of round mouths and protruding eyes. The little mackerel are like children that want only to play and let themselves be pulled by the current. The small sharks are serious adults, full of grave thoughts. Later there began the parade of the fishes he recognized, having drawn them in the sand. The old man was right; they all existed, moving about, displacing others, turning around one another like a modern-day parade.

10.

Juan sat up feeling his legs numb. The float continued to bob up and down. The silence was broken only by the intermittent "pluf-plaf" of the breaking waves.

The old man, with his hat down over his eyes, once again prepared the fish hooks with great care, as if time had ceased to exist. I wonder if he's hungry? Surely he must be thirsty. What could he be thinking deep in his heart?

"What are you thinking about, don Andrés?"

He had never dared to pose that question.

The old man is like the sea. What does the sea think? It probably thinks about its inhabitants and how to feed that huge number. If he could choose, he would choose to live in the sea, not like the mariners, but like the fish.

The old man did not like to navigate. He never went fishing aboard the ship. When he was invited— they no longer invited him now—he would answer:

"I'm going to the rocks."

Ultimately, Juan had accustomed himself to wait.

It is necessary to contemplate the breathing of the sea. The birds breathe, men breathe, fish breathe, the sea breathes. The rocks do not breathe, nor does the earth. The sea at times breathes in an agitated way, like an animal that is tired of running. At that time it seemed to be playing with sea breezes.

There are fishes with small bodies, like mackerel and the roncadors. Others have large bodies, like the black corvines, the seawolves, the sharks, the eels and, of course, the whales. The sea has an immense body. The sea's body is melded into the ends of the earth.

"Tell me, don Andrés, is there a body that does not occupy space? No space at all, that can squeeze through any space, like the air? Is there such a body?"

Of course, before asking him that question, he would have to tell him about those "adults" who had asked his help before he had arrived at the dunes.

11.

One morning in the early summer Chuno went to look for him at the ranch. The uncle slept a drunken sleep and Juan had disappeared. At about noon, he found him at a corner. He told him that the boys wanted to see him, that they had a small job for him, that they needed him. Chuno winked his eye the way older people do.

Juan's heart leapt with joy.

His uncle had him at the ranch, that is, he let him spend the night in a corner. During the day he would fool around and roam about. He was too small to join his elders at the bars, so he just came and went. Like a street urchin, totally free, free and alone.

Juan played ball quite well. He loved long games that seemed never to finish. If it were up to him, he would play from dawn until dusk. He never tired. He had limitless energy to jump, run, roll on the ground, for he was small and light.

Ball games filled him with a strange fascination: He'd receive blows, but seemed not to get hurt; he would evade the ball, slip on it, evade and escape from it. At times, just for a moment, he would try to tame it: The ball became docile, obedient, following his feet that ran like the devil until, receiving a signal, flashed across the opposite court leaving the boy reaching for the air.

Juan did not speak during a game and very little at other times. There was no use yelling at the ball: it was deaf and dumb. One had to guess its intentions and go after it at full speed because it constantly changed its aim, its goals. The player had to be attentive and able to concentrate.

To be called by his elders was like being called by the President of the Republic. Adults belong to a desired, and yet feared, world. To penetrate that world he had to be big and his body refused to grow rapidly. Juan would measure himself on the wall of the ranch. He had drawn a line with a nail at the level of his head. Months passed and the line remained the same, perhaps because when he first marked the wall he had cheated by standing on tiptoe.

And now, adults wanted to see him!

Juan, with his heart beating rapidly, made a gesture of indifference as if saying: "I'm really bored that these adults are calling me at all hours." He did not ask any questions. He concentrated. He could not afford to make a mistake; but, beware, the ball is inconstant and capricious: it leaps and rebounds at will.

When he thought deeply, Juan used to sink his head between his shoulders making him appear even smaller. Chuno took him to a bare piece of land next to the football field. Three adults were lying about in a section that was grassy and lush. Of the four he knew only Chuno and Zurdo. The others were not from the neighborhood.

"This is Flea."

In the area everyone knew Flea.

They watched him warily.

"We want you to climb this tree."

Zurdo knew very well that Juan could climb like a cat. He wanted him to show off before the others. Juan in two leaps stood on the top uppermost branches of the tree. Then another man spoke, a thin, dark-skinned man with long arms who was a stranger to him.

"Come on down," said a soft, almost feminine voice. "We have some business to discuss with you."

Juan hurried down and stood by the trunk of the tree. His heart was pounding. "The older people" were speaking to him about business, about important things; they needed him.

"Tonight we have to do some moving. We need you to open the gate at the end of the street."

The tall young man paused to observe him. Juan remained still and thoughtful.

"We need you to climb a tree like this one, to run through the branches up to the cornice and to climb through a small half-opened window. Are you willing?"

He nodded his head affirmatively.

"Once inside comes the most difficult part. To

climb the tree you need your legs; inside the house you need your head."

He paused waiting for a reaction. The boy said nothing.

"You have to get to the front door and open it. If you're caught, you're lost. Are you afraid?"

"No." His voice was strong. Why should he be afraid? It's only when he's in the house that he needs to think hard.

"The first part of the plan depends on you. We'll be waiting outside." The four adults were going to depend on him.

"They need me, they need me, I can't fail them."

Later they spoke to him about the loot and how they'd share it. Juan was distracted. He was feeling a new sensation, marvelous, tender....

Without saying a word, he went away with his hands inside the torn pockets of his pants.

They showed him the small window of the first floor, the tree, the branch, the cornice. He would have to walk along the cornice close to the wall like a hornet. One of the adults stood in one corner, Chuno was in the other. The signal was given: all was calm. The thin one with the high voice showed him the tree, calling him to action.

Juan climbed with bare feet, walked along the branch and from there to the cornice. The cornice was wider than he had expected. The small window was open, he put in his head, his shoulders, jumped quietly and landed on his feet on a cold tile.

Now was the moment when everything depended on him. The adults were waiting one behind the other smoking cigarettes.

At that precise moment Juan had a revelation: he

realized that the adults with their long arms and legs, with all their great strength, needed his small, light body. They were stuck to the ground, they lived resting against the wall and against trees, they played football some of the time and got out of breath like beaten dogs. He, on the other hand, jumped and rebounded like a ball, walked on his hands as well as on his feet and could be supported by a thin branch.

Perhaps then it was not good to grow. When his head surpassed the mark on the wall at the ranch, he would no longer be able to climb trees or walk along cornices or go through small windows.

He touched his body. Thank you, legs! Thank you arms! You have done a good job! Everyone depends on you. Now I need you, head. See if you can be as good as my arms and legs.

He found himself in the bathroom on the second floor. He would look for the stairs to get to the first floor. Juan stood by the half-opened door. His body took up very little space like a cat's. How interesting it would be to have a body that did not occupy any space! No space at all! That could squeeze through half-opened doors, even through keyholes... Concentrate, head, concentrate.

He found himself in a huge dining room, larger than his uncle's entire ranch. The adults had given him a flashlight. He turned it on. He saw three doors, all ajar. The floor was made of wood and made small noises when he walked. Juan peeked through the first door: the kitchen. He looked through the second: two beds and someone sleeping. The third door was the bathroom. Where were the stairs? Come now, head, guide my legs, concentrate like when you play football.

Maybe the kitchen has another door. Yes, but it faced a terrace that had no exit.

Then you must cross the room. This idea made him happy. No adult could cross the room with his heavy body without making a loud noise and waking everyone up. He, on the other hand, trusted his legs that could walk almost without touching the ground. Truly, he trusted his legs much more than his head. His errors at football were never caused by his legs but by his head which failed to understand the ball. On the other hand, when the ball was in touch with his feet it was as docile as a puppy.

On the bed slept such a big man that his feet stuck out beyond the bed. He was curious. He went near to see him closer. Yes, he was an adult, like Chuno, but much bigger. A giant!

The other door, half opened, faced a wooden staircase. The steps squeaked more than the floor of the dining room or the bedroom. How wonderful it would be to have a body that did not weigh anything, as light as a balloon!

The staircase led him to the front door. The key was in the door and he turned it twice.

Immediately he felt someone turning the knob from outside, but the door wouldn't open.

"Flea," called a voice, low and high-pitched.

"Here I am."

"Look for the bolt near the door."

Of course, the bolt was locked. He pulled up. It didn't move. Come, arms, don't let my legs get ahead of you. He grabbed it with both hands, breathed deeply, and pulled again. It gave in. Again they pulled the door from the outside. But it didn't open.

"The lock up above," whispered the same voice.

He needed a chair to reach the lock up above. He crossed over to another door and entered a living room with large chairs and a piano. He saw the piano stool and lifted it up carefully.

Ugh, it was heavy! He could not afford to stumble, much less to fall. Juan had full confidence in his legs. They led him straight to the door without stumbling. He climbed on the bench and with his arms extended grabbed the lock. He pulled without success. He tried again with all his might, careful not to make noise. But he was too light. A short while ago he was wishing he were as light as a balloon. Now he wished he were stronger, or simply an adult. He began to swing on the bolt, his feet in the air. His arms began to hurt. Finally it flew open with a bang!

The noise was like the explosion of a bomb. It resounded through the living room, it flew up the stairs, filled the upper floor, went out through the windows and echoed around the neighborhood.

It was an interminable noise, echoing in the night. The boy remained frozen to the floor, waiting for the storm to cease. He could hear the men outside running on the cobblestones down the block.

Little by little, silence again reigned in the house. There were no footsteps, no screams or gunshots.

Then Juan stood up, lifted the bench, replaced it by the piano and waited for the arrival of an adult.

He waited a long time. He heard the chimes of a clock and then he went to sleep.

When it got lighter outside he opened the door with the hopes of seeing Chuno. There was no one in the street. The adults had run away. He alone had fulfilled his mission, but he didn't receive the recompense he expected. The adults did not appreciate his work.

He felt hungry, but not sleepy. He kicked an empty preserves jar against the molding of the sidewalk. What a difference with a ball! The ball is made to be agile, fun to use. The best invention ever made!

12.

The float on his line began to raise its little red head: it rose and rested, rose and rested...

Juan grabbed the rod with both hands. Concentrate, concentrate! The float began a giddy descent to the bottom of the sea. A sudden tug. Not too brusque, and the rod bent over, pulled by an inhabitant of the ocean.

"That one down there is not a baby. It must be an adult."

He stood up on the rock leaning the line against his breast. The adult swam further out.

"No! You can't get away. I have you tied down."

Then it swam toward the coastline. The line scraped against the edge of a rock.

"Ah! You're trying to cut my line? You are an intelligent fish! You have good legs and a good head. My head is not as good as my legs."

The fish stopped moving, caught perhaps in some underground grotto.

"I'm not going to pull hard! I'll wait until you come out of your cave. I'm in no hurry. Don't you know the old man taught me to wait? Look, it's six in the evening and we've been here since early morning. You see? Without eating, without speaking. The old man must be happy with me."

He looked at him from the corner of his eye: The old man sat still, his hat pushed way back as he watched the gyration of the sun around the earth. He didn't turn once to watch him. Juan no longer needed advice, but he did need the old man to answer some few questions:

"Why does the fisherman go into unknown places? Fish never invade the earth or play tricks on men...."

Why, if he is a beggar, does the fisherman grab at alms like a thief taking advantage of the deceit of his bait?"

At that moment, with his rod tense and leaning back, Juan was the happiest boy in the world.

The fish began to wiggle.

"One, two, three, one, two, three...."

"And now what?"

A great idea crossed his mind. The fish was inviting him to visit him in his house. He was saying:

"Let's go, Flea. Don't be afraid. Come so I can show you where I live, introduce you to my wife, my children and also my in-laws... One, two, three...."

"No, I can't go, Mr. Fish. In your house I would drown. We are different: I belong on land. Do you understand?"

Perhaps the fish at the end of the line was a great sargo. The sargos never stick their heads above water and thus they think that everyone is like them, that everyone can breathe under the water. Maybe they think that the only thing that exists is their aquatic world.

29

The old man had explained to him that fishes breathe like humans, but in the water. Out of the water they drown...Ah! If he had a diver's suit at that moment, he could accept the fish's invitation.

"One, two, three..."

All bodies breathe. All living bodies; the sea, the fishes, humans, an ant... The rock has a dead body, that's why it doesn't breathe. On earth there are many dead bodies; in the sea everything is alive.

"But what about those who have drowned, don Andrés?"

"A good question, boy, a good question," responded the old man.

The drowned are dead bodies, that's why the sea always returns them to the shore. For example, a man drowns way out there, by the horizon, see? Well then, after a few days you will find him here at your feet, by the shore. The sea does not contain any cemeteries.

"The sea contains no cemeteries," a phrase Juan continued to think about for a long time. A thought full of light, like the silvery fish of the sea that shone on the sand during the night.

He decided never to exchange empires again. He wanted to be a disciple of an empire where cemeteries did not exist.

"Why, don Andrés, did your friend Romualdo die if he was a friend of the sea?"

The old man told him that he was a victim of enemies. He had died on the land, the Empire of Cemeteries.

"One, two, three, one, two, three..."

The fish called him insistently, it invited him again and again and would accept no excuses. His legs and arms were concentrated on the task, but his head was lost in a shining memory.

13.

It had been a year, or so the old man reminded him, that he had decided to leave, to abandon his neighborhood. He had never seen the sea. He would go in search of it.

The idea came to him during a football game, and it left him stunned. He lost his concentration completely: the ball seemed to elude him continually, to make fun of him. He didn't care. His teammates insulted him. He still didn't care.

For many days he had felt a new sensation of something marvelous that was waiting for him; but he didn't know what it was until that moment.

On the following morning, very early, he left his uncle's ranch and walked to the station. He had no money to pay his fare; he would hitch a ride, perhaps latch on to a projection like he used to do on the bus. The train arrived with the usual screeching noise made when it ground to a halt. The boy got on a crowded car. He was hidden by the crowd. Through a small slit, he could see the blue sky. The train whistle sounded three times and then the cars began to pull out of the station.

Juan felt something strange, marvelous. Something he had never before experienced. Later he would learn that what he felt is called joy.

He travelled for many hours. He felt hunger, cold, thirst. He slept on the floor, eluded conductors;

walked aimlessly through stations, changed trains three times. He never spoke or asked anyone any questions.

On the third day he arrived at the coast.

It was dawn.

He walked down a wide, reddish path, the path of his dreams. He walked slowly. The air was for him something totally new and intoxicating. There was no black soil along the coast as he had dreamed, but instead sand that was fine and white or yellow (Juan did not know what to call that color); and the trees had open branches at the top.

After two kilometers, the road came to an end. Between two hills of sand, he saw for the first time the perfect green of the sea.

Juan walked on through a small valley formed by the dunes until he could get a broad view of the sea and its limitless coastline.

He was overcome by the immensity of it all. It was true what they said: The sea extends to the horizon. The sun was beginning to rise from the depths of the ocean. Nothing greater could exist than the sea. Nothing could exist more brilliant than the sun.

He lay on the sand with his eyes closed. From time to time he would open them to fill himself with that green, the greenest in the world.

He felt small, insignificant. In the presence of the sea adults were as small as he. Everything was small, even lions and elephants. All of them could drown, disappear—men, animals, houses and even the tallest skyscrapers.

Later he got up and ran until he became exhausted.

He threw himself on the sand and shouted:

"I want to be your friend, I want to be your friend, I want to be your friend..."

Did the sea have friends? To Juan it seemed friendly.

He rolled along the dunes and then began to run again with all the strength his legs could afford him until he reached the water's edge. He wanted to touch it. The water was cold, but not very. A wave covered his foot with foam.

"Mr. Sea, Mr. Sea, Mr. Sea..." Juan ran along the shore splashing his body. He ran and ran. His heart leapt with joy, with emotion, with surprise.

Where did the sea have its eyes? Where its ears? Perhaps it could see from all over and even hear the murmur of one's thoughts.

"Mr. Sea, Mr. Sea," he thought without parting his lips. Certainly the sea could also hear thoughts. Without doubt it was not necessary to shout.

"I am Juan. In my neighborhood they call me Flea. I don't like to be called Flea, but they say it anyway. I play football very well. I have good arms and legs, but my head is a little weak. I don't want to go back to my neighborhood; I want to stay near you. Will you let me?"

Exhausted from running, he dropped on the wet sand feeling a salty taste in his mouth.

Would he someday become the sea's friend? One can never become friends with another in just a few minutes. To know another requires time. From that moment they would begin to know each other. What would he have to do to get to know the sea?

For the first time he wanted to be a fish so he could travel inside the ocean. Maybe if he got very quiet he might hear the voice of the sea. He would have to become quiet inside. Concentrate and not think of anything.

When he awakened the sun was in the middle of the sky. The sea had changed completely: milky, covered with braids of whiteness. In the morning it had been a man, now it was a woman... How awful to call the sea a woman! When anyone called him a little girl, he would fight until he had no more strength left. Nevertheless, he had not wanted to insult the sea. Juan was all mixed up. His head confused him and thrust him into difficult straits. He would have to be very careful with his head.

Where could the morning sea have gone? Perhaps he ought to introduce himself again to this white sea with braids.

"My name is Juan. In my neighborhood they call me Flea..."

He didn't know whether to call the sea Sir or Madam... Because women, too, must get mad if someone calls them boys... In any case this sea was less solemn, more playful and merry.

If the sea hears me, if it accepts me as close to it, it will feed me. If it doesn't like me, I prefer to die of hunger.

"Mrs. Sea, I'm hungry. I'm also thirsty."

He had never felt so happy. Never in all his life. Happier even than in the morning when he had first arrived. He had slept on the sand. He had not had fears or nightmares. And now he had discovered how he would know if the sea was listening to him.

At nightfall when the sun was beginning to hide behind the dunes, Juan met the old man. He ate in the shack and slept in a new and marvelous country, one he had reached after three days' travel on a train.

14.

One, two, three... One, two, three...

The fish kept calling him like an impatient telegraph operator. The fishing rod was doubled over, pointed in, firmly set against his stomach; his firm arms and his strong legs were set against the rock. The fish moved about three times and then rested.

"I can't come down, Mr. Fish. I can't visit your house. I am an inhabitant of the land and I cannot jump into the sea or I'll drown. I would need a breathing device which we don't have. Do you understand?"

Then the line was cut. Juan reeled. The rod jumped for a moment and then recovered its position of stillness. He contemplated for a moment the line cut against the sharp edge of the rock.

"Oh, Mr. Fish," he exclaimed in admiration, "you have a firmer head than mine. I let myself be deceived by your insistent call. I completely lost my concentration."

He sat on the reef to change the line. Smiling, he was thinking:

"I'm happy, Mr. Fish, that you have beaten me. Very happy." A good fisherman rejoices when the fish triumphs. Juan was now a good fisherman.

"His wife must now be taking the bait out of his mouth with great care and in a short time he'll be recounting his adventures to his friends. I congratulate you, Mr. Fish."

15.

The sun was at his back. It gave him warmth but without the force of noonday. The milky sea with its silver braids had disappeared. The green sea reigned supreme without blemish and with white foam. The waves had grown taller. They dashed against the rock with greater energy, inundating the fishing gear and wetting the feet of the fishermen. Some small clouds were gathering above the horizon to the southwest. If they become dark, they will herald bad weather that night. No! During those days the moon would swallow the storms.

"The sun is male and stands firm," the old man explained to him, "but the one who gives orders is the moon which is female. She controls the rain and the drought, orients the fishes in their travels, directs the tides and the height of the waters and many other things that we don't know."

Since the sargo had cut the line on the edge of the rock, two hours had passed. The knapsacks were as empty as their stomachs, but Juan was enjoying himself because soon he would be a disciple of the sea.

"What does it mean to be a disciple, don Andrés?"

"Do you instruct the sea?"

"No."

"Does the sea instruct you?"

"Yes."

"Then you are a disciple of the sea."

Juan felt proud. No one could have a master that

was more noble, richer, more powerful, one that would never die...

Up until that moment he had never had a teacher. Football he had learned to play by himself. His uncle was never a teacher. Nor any other adult either.

Fishing is totally different from football, he said to himself. In football the legs play a prominent role; in fishing, on the other hand, the primacy rests with the head, with its thoughts. In football everything depends on oneself: The ball is always at the reach of the foot. In fishing, everything depends on the sea.

"Fishing is the only way to get to know the sea," said the old man. "Fishing from the breakers or from the pier on stormy days."

Juan had learned that waiting meant at times dreaming, at times remembering.

He remembered...

16.

He remembered that that night had been charged with electricity. It had been a sultry day with an implacable north wind which lasted until the sun set. The sands circled around alleys by the force of the wind. By the end of the day the configurations of the dunes had changed.

The night brought a gentle calm and a smooth sea with small waves which touched the sand some few meters away and returned home again. That tranquil sea reflected life through a strange, phosphorescent glow, a foam of stars.

Juan contemplated the luminous sea, a sea that was different in the morning than in the afternoon. The sky was illumined by great bolts of lightning: Rays of fire in zigzag shapes that stretched across the valleys of the heavens.

The old man had stayed home mending a shirt while Juan left to walk along the shore. Stormy nights provoked in him wonder and fear at the same time. The wonder brought him to the seashore, the fear caused him to stay near the house.

In a while there would fall a torrential rain. The thunder could still be heard from afar. When he felt the first drops he would return and fall asleep with the winds howling in his ears.

He sat on the sand with the sea and the storm before him. Beyond the phosphorescence there reigned the night. Juan centered his vision. At night, when nobody can see anything, what happens in the sea? Do the fish sleep? Briefly the lightning reveals the mystery: all is calm, all is empty. He thought he perceived a black stain in the distance: A boat, a boat that was sailing without any lights; or one of those nocturnal islands that hide under the water during the day.

He felt very small, like the day he first saw the sea, when he walked along the path that led him from the station to the shore. The immense sky, the immense sea, the immense night, the gigantic storm and the lightning so capable of illuminating all the immensities. Lost on the beach and in the night, Juan felt like a small grain of sand, a tiny piece of dust, abandoned, unrecognized...

Poor Flea, pretentious Flea, conceited enough to think he could wrest the secrets of the nocturnal sea.

He got up and started home. The shack, the old man, all insignificant. Men have solid brick houses, houses of stone, with strong foundations set by machinery that raises columns of cement. (When he used to live in his old neighborhood, he spent hours watching the hoisting machines at work.) They, on the other hand, had a little house made of wooden slats poorly put together where sand slipped through on windy days.

They were at the mercy of the sea, of the night, of the storms.

Once again a flash of lightning revealed the tranquil surface of the sea. He seemed to see a bundle a few meters from the shore, as if it were a buoy. He waited for another flash of light. Yes, there was a bundle rocking a few feet from where he stood. Curiosity impelled his legs, and without hesitation he ran into the water.

The incline by the coast was pronounced. Immediately he was up to his chest in water. If he were older, he thought, the water would reach to his waist. The sky became brighter and he saw the bundle a little to the right and closer to the shore.

Juan walked slowly.

"Sir Ocean, be good to me and let me reach the bundle."

The black stain seemed to be balancing on its side; but it seemed to lack the energy needed to move closer.

"The coastline is treacherous, full of holes. If you're not careful, you'll slip into one," explained the old man.

And especially at night, he thought.

"Mr. Sea, be good, pull the bundle over to me."

This time the sea heard his prayer. The bundle began to move and Juan reached it with his short arms and dragged it toward the shore.

The first drops began to fall, big fat drops separated one from the other. Juan ran along the beach and headed home. He ran as if someone were chasing him. He arrived, together with a thunderclap that announced a huge downpour.

He entered dripping water and stopped at the door with the bundle in hand. He looked at the shack as if seeing it for the first time. He wanted to engrave in his mind every detail so as to remember it faithfully without forgetting anything.

A lamp suspended from a hook near the door shone brightly. Next to the northeastern wall, the one most protected from the great storms of the south, he saw the two boards that served him as a bed. That wall held the only window in the little house and was kept closed by some boards held in place with iron hooks. At dawn the house was bathed in rays of light that filtered in through the hinges. Across a slit in the window a friendly ray of light passed through to Juan and played across his body before he rose. The southeast wall was covered with lines, fishing rods of all sizes, floats and sinkers. On the wall opposite the door there was a collection of rods held in place by bent nails. On the left of the entrance on the northeast wall hung two pots and one frying pan. A small wooden table and a brazier that they lit on wintry days served as kitchen. The ceiling was made of braided straw with a slope from south to north. Four beams supported the reeds that protected them from the cold and the heat.

"The shack is dark," thought Juan, "and nevertheless it is filled with joy; it is small and the sea fits within it; it is fragile but there is no safer place on earth... On the coast, I was weak like a grain of sand; now I am a firm rock.

Seated on a stool, his back resting against a corrugated wooden beam, with his hands resting upon his knees and his head lowered, don Andrés was dozing.

Juan contemplated him calmly, forgetting about his soaked clothes and the mysterious bundle. Gray hair, long face, leathery skin with a thousand wrinkles, hands that are strong, large, long-suffering and hard-working...Tall, muscular, without an ounce of fat.

Don Andrés never complained; but at the end of the day he felt tired, fatigued... I wonder how old he is. 70, 80, 100?... Some day the old man will die near the sea. Two tears ran down his cheeks and mixed with the water of the rain and the sea.

"Don Andrés, look what I pulled out of the sea..."

The old man lifted his head and stared at the bundle without saying anything. He got up and pulled out an old towel from a drawer near his bed.

"Dry yourself, boy, and change your clothes."

Juan dropped the bundle, dried himself and changed his clothes. Meanwhile, don Andrés poured out a little blue alcohol, struck a match near to it and a small flame began to heat the burner. The storm had arrived accompanied by fire and water. The rainfall resonated in the house and the rain soaked the slits in the window and walls. The old man blew on the flame until it leapt, blue and trembling. Then he placed a pot over the fire.

"I'm going to open the bundle," said Juan.

The external wrapping was made of oilcloth.

With his small penknife he began to cut through cloth as his hands shook; but he did not want to display any haste, much less emotion.

The old man stirred the pot.

"Tell me, boy, what do you think of having some *chupin*?"

"Fantastic!"

When finally Juan succeeded in undoing the cloth, he could not repress a cry of admiration.

"Look, don Andrés."

The bundle contained a small portfolio (similar to an executive's attaché case) covered with another material supported by two small aluminum balls like those children use on the beach. The bundle was prepared so it could float. The old man did not stop stirring the contents of the pot.

"Those floats would be good for our swimming classes, don Andrés."

"You no longer need floats."

The old man had given him several lessons. Juan learned with great ease. His legs, as usual, served him well. In swimming, as in football, his legs and arms played roles of protagonists.

"Breathing, boy, is very important. Turn your head just enough to stick your nose above water and turn back into the water like a fish." Juan moved about very much in his element; but the old man would not let him go in too deeply beyond the sand dunes. What could there be inside the valise?

"The oilcloth will be useful." Don Andrés did not explain what for.

The seams were very strong and Juan's penknife had no effect.

"Don Andrés, will you lend me your knife?"

42

"Here, take it."

Juan took it out of its leather case and began to cut; but his hands were trembling too much. He abandoned the knife and waited.

The fish was hot. The old man took out two plates made of shiny tin from the drawer and served two portions. Juan put into place a shelf that served as a table, covered it with a small red tablecloth, placed two glasses, bread and a bottle of wine on it. And they sat in front of this, face to face, as was their custom. From the first day the old man had taught him how to set the table and how to eat "like civilized people." Juan enjoyed the ritual which he fulfilled to the letter. And when storms beat upon the shack, then the dinner hour took on a special beauty.

Their solitude was complete, separated as they were by the tempest and the roaring winds from all else. The shack was transformed into an island of six square meters, nailed, as it reached its perfection. Juan was dragged beyond time and set down in the midst of the very heart of things. When the storm would pass, he would return to the surface, like an ancient vessel abandoning the depths of the sea.

Nevertheless, that night the small satchel interrupted the ritual and muffled their communication.

"Don Andrés, what do you suppose is in the bag?"

"Papers."

Juan felt betrayed.

"What are papers for?"

The old man shrugged his shoulders.

"It's a gift that the sea has given us, don Andrés," he stated.

17.

The red buoy bobbed up and down nodding its head. Every now and again Juan would pull the line from the water to clean off the algae and check on the bait.

To wait is to recall.

To recall means to relive what has been lived and to understand it better. Recalling is the digestion made by the head. Certain things happened to him that required rethinking after long hours to be able to realize what they meant. At times it was hard to recall with exactitude.

At that moment, he said: "It's a gift from the sea." But his head seemed once again to confuse him. The old man made no comment. Why didn't the old man tell him he was mistaken?

He always put away their table and cleaned the plates and the pot with sand. Meanwhile the old man would be smoking his pipe. That time it was different.

"Go back to your bundle, boy," he said. "Tonight I'll take care of the dishes."

On the way home he would ask him:

"Why didn't you correct me, don Andrés, and warn me about the risk I was taking." Juan took up again his struggle with the oilcloth. The knife bent time and again against the taut covering of the package like a stiff guitar string. A gust of wind of hurricane force rocked the shack. The lamp suspended from a wire swung back and forth. The old man murmured something unintelligible.

Ras! The point of the knife cut the material.

44

With impatient hands he finished cutting the cloth leaving exposed a case covered in thick nylon. With the knife he perforated the plastic and, finally, he had in his hands a black valise.

"Look, don Andrés!"

A violent clap of thunder silenced him.

The valise was closed with two bronze latches. He pulled them open. The lamplight illuminated the inside that was stuffed with bundles of bills. Each bundle was wrapped with a strip of white paper. The bills were green and all marked with the number 100.

Juan took a bundle and handed it to the old man. The latter brought it over close to the lamp which had not ceased to rock back and forth, and then he came back.

"Money. Dollars."

"Money?"

"A lot of money."

"What are dollars?"

"American money. It's worth more than ours. From this moment you're rich."

"We're rich, don Andrés, we two, you and I."

"No, boy, I don't want that money. I don't need it. I'm all right as I am..."

The old man finished drying the pot which he hung on a hook and then shook the crumbs off the tablecloth. He placed the board by his bed while the wind howled and strained through the grooves in the walls. He studied the movements of the lamp, felt the beams with his large hand and commented:

"Tomorrow I'll reinforce the beams of the south wall. The winds are loosening them."

Juan was sticking his hand between the bundles of bills, the black valise still on his knees. Why did

45

the old man say: "Tomorrow I'll tighten the beams on the south wall?" Why didn't he say, as he usually did, from the night he had arrived in the little house, "Tomorrow, boy, we will reinforce the beams on the south wall." Juan would turn the tourniquet with a rusty iron pipe, while the old man would lean against the wall from the inside.

"Now, boy, now! Harder! Use more strength!"

Later, together, they would contemplate the work.

"If we ignore the beams, the winds will lift us up like comets," he used to say.

"What things can I buy with this money?"

"Whatever you want: a house, a car, a boat... Whatever you want."

Don Andrés touched the window, wrapped himself up in his blanket and threw himself on the straw mattress.

"Good-bye, boy. When you go to bed put out the lamp."

The old man left him alone with his valise full of paper and his thoughts tied up in knots. He did not offer to help him untie the knots. He put out the lamp. He watched as the wick gradually lost its light until it became part of the reigning darkness.

He threw himself on the straw mattress. The shack lighted up from time to time with the lightning caused by the storm. The roar of the ocean seemed to intensify from time to time. The noise from the sea is different. The old man had taught him to distinguish its tones and recognize their significance. When he went out for a stroll amid the calm waters, the sound was like a soft drumming on the sand: the affectionate sea. From time to time a huge wave hit the shore: the sighing sea, or the sea that was shaking off sleep, according to the hour of the day. At that moment it was the angry sea; although the sea never got angry. If it did, it would cover the land and goodbye house, roads, trains, telephone poles, wires... But the sea knows its limits and respects them... It is never angry for real.

Pay attention, head! Concentrate on this bag! The old man told you you were rich. I can buy a ball, a pair of shoes, a shirt and pants. But the old man needs shoes too, and at least a new shirt...

Why didn't the old man want that? Being rich means much more than buying a pair of shoes. He could buy a car, a boat... The old man didn't like boats.

His uncle dreamed of being rich. Older people robbed to get money. He didn't have to steal; the sea gave him a suitcase full of bills.

The shopkeeper had told him his uncle was a miser who had money stashed away. Juan never found out where it was hidden. Neither did he ever find out if he really had money hidden on the ranch. Everyone wants to be rich. People kill for money. "The world spins around dollars." Where did he learn that expression that was now spinning through his head?

Suddenly his mind lit up with a brilliance stronger than the lightning of the storm. It was a vision of continual light that showed him himself leading the life of a rich young man. In the first place no one would call him Flea. He would go about well-dressed; he would eat what he felt like eating, he wouldn't have to live on his uncle's ranch... He grabbed the valise.

What would he be like rich? Who would he be?

18.

He dreamed of a road that was zigzagging around bare hills. From time to time it passed alongside miserable shacks piled one upon the other.

Juan was driving a splendid car. His legs, always agile, coordinated the movement on the pedals, while his eyes followed the line on the asphalt road. His arms obeyed the movement of his eyes with the simple pressure of his fingers on the steering wheel.

Nevertheless, in spite of the anatomically perfect seat which accommodated perfectly his small body, he felt the exhaustion of the kilometers. For hours he had been looking for a place to stop to eat, to rest and then continue on his way. He turned the wheel once more and saw before him a high-rise hotel surrounded by huge trees which were very different from the weak, thin shrubbery that could be found in the desert.

A parking lot in the sun opened its cement arms to him. He got out of the car and was careful to lock the door. He walked toward the main entrance of the building and went through a revolving door which brought him a breath of cold air. He walked on a pale red rug which led to a glass double door that faced a dining room of many tables and waiters with white gloves. He sat down at a table that had a red tablecloth and was near a window.

Immediately he was approached by a man with a tan mustache and impeccable attire.

"What do you want, boy?"

"I want to eat."

"Get out of here or I'll have you put in jail."

Juan, without batting an eye (how often had he not lived this scene?) pulled a bag of bills out of his pocket and placed it on the table.

"Oh, sir, forgive me." The man bowed with respect and left.

"Flea" was still wearing his usual clothes: a mended pair of pants of unknown color which reached to the calves of his legs, threadbare shirt, and sandals so full of holes that his toes came through.

With soft steps a waiter approached, a man short and chubby and middle-aged. The mustached fellow must have sent him to take care of serving him.

"You have money," he said. He shrugged his shoulders and added. "The rich sometimes like to disguise themselves like poor people. What would you like, sir?"

Juan, staring out the window, asked, "Tell me, where is the sea?"

"Far from here. You have to follow that road."

"Do you know don Andrés?"

"Don Andrés?" he repeated, surprised.

"A fisherman..."

"No... The fish comes here in refrigerated cars. You can eat it fresh as if it came right out of the water. We have all kinds. For example, I can offer you shrimp a la marinara."

"Don't you miss the sea?"

"Well," the man seemed puzzled, "I'm from around here. I've never been near the sea."

"That doesn't matter. I invite you, come with me and we can go together in search of the sea."

"Thank you, sir, but I'm not up to any adventures. I have a wife and children to feed."

"Wouldn't you like to become a disciple of the sea?"

"I don't understand." The waiter left, placing the napkin over his arm to take care of other, less complicated guests.

How many days had passed by now on that interminable trip? Juan had lost count.

"Waiter," he called.

"Yes, sir."

Juan put a bill in his hand. The man bowed profoundly.

"Thank you very much, sir, thank you."

"What day is today?"

"Sunday, sir, Sunday, the 24th of January."

"The 24th of January? What year?"

"The year 2001. Don't you remember the celebrations at the close of the millennium?"

Then have I been travelling with this confounded bag for a year and have never reached the sea, he thought.

"What is your name?"

"Rodolfo, sir, here to serve you."

"Tell me, Rodolfo, all those cars in that parking lot full of suitcases, some in trailers, where are they going?"

"To the beach for a vacation."

"How long will it take them to get there?"

"Well, it depends on the speed they go at and the number of stops they make."

"More or less," said Juan impatiently.

"A couple of days."

The usual answer. He had been traveling exactly a year to get to the sea which always seemed to be two days away.

"Rodolfo, why can't I get to that place that everyone else is going to?"

"Table 17," shouted the voice of the mustached man.

"Pardon me, sir, they're calling me." Rodolfo got up with haste.

When Juan first decided to abandon the neighborhood and leave for the sea, he had arrived in three days at the dunes and that night he found the little house. Now it seemed impossible for him. He had been traveling without interruption for a year. He saw all different landscapes and always found himself two days' journey from the sea. For a whole year he had been unable to fish by the breakers.

His heart was heavy as he thought about the happiness he had lost. For a year he had searched for the little house on the dunes and always he came to large, solid cement buildings. What curse had descended upon him? His head could not figure it out and neither could his legs which carried him without direction or enthusiasm.

His memories brought back a conversation.

"How lazy I feel getting back to work. The beach is divine."

"Stella learned water skiing."

The voices came to him from a table behind his shoulders. He listened carefully: they were bringing him news of the sea.

"The first day she was as red as a lobster."

"Don't you know what it was...!"

"We were fishing on the high seas."

"We were on Paco's yacht."

"A dream of a ship!"

"You must have had some life aboard!"

51

"Indiscreet!" Laughter.

"Well, on the beach it's so crowded that you can't even walk."

The window next to Juan reflected the table: eight persons, three men and five women.

"I assure you, you can't find room in any hotel."

"We made a reservation a year ago."

"For how much?"

"Sixty dollars a day."

"Robbers; they ask whatever they want."

"Don't forget to ask for a dish of *chez*."

"It's the most delicious seafood platter I've ever eaten."

Could it be possible that those people might bring him news of the sea? About its color, its changing tides, the movement of the fishes, the noise made by the breakers, its solitude, the nocturnal lights and its apparitions.

Is it possible that they might have seen don Andrés with his hat down over his eyes, and his long, wrinkled, strong hands?

On the window glass, as on a magic screen, the men and women at the table behind him seemed to mesh with the leaves of trees, with a child playing with a bicycle wheel, the artificial turf in the park, the pool...

What joy! In two days, they'll be lying in the sun...

Two days...the sea was always two days away. For a whole year he had been listening to the same chant. Perhaps the sea was annoyed with him and didn't want to see him, it was eluding him. If he walked north, the sea flowed south, if he walked toward the east, the sea flowed toward the setting sun...

"Sea, immense sea, my friend the sea, where are you? Why do you flee from me? I have been looking for you a whole year, day and night..."

His throat became tight. Concentrate, head, concentrate. In his mind he could hear the words he had heard:

"You can't find room in any hotel."

"The beach is so crowded, you can't walk."

"The first day I got as red as a lobster."

"A ship like you see in the movies was shining like the hall at home..."

Concentrate, head, concentrate. Listen, and please stop thinking...

His sea, the old man's sea was a sea of solitary dunes. They used to walk alone; once in a while another fisherman might pass by. They never saw multitudes on the sand. Neither were there roulette games or shiny ships...

Then he understood why his neighbors at the table near him did not give him any news of the sea; they did not come from his sea. They did not know it.

Instantly he lost interest in his trip. It was no longer important to get to that beach, or to continue on that road. He went out with trembling steps from the air conditioning to the noonday heat. A terrible thought crossed his mind; a thought so terrible that it caused his legs to weaken, legs that had always been the strongest part of his body.

What if the sea doesn't exist? If the old man doesn't exist? If the little house on the dunes is but a dream?

What if there are only vacationers with bronzed

bodies going and coming in beautiful cars? If there exists only that anonymous sea, the sea of tourists with anonymous fish, with fishermen who fish just to kill time, with boats that cruise along the water and submarines that move along underneath...? What if there is just a sea without eyes, or ears, without heart or nobility?

If his sea did not exist, Juan was but a dot lost in a world that comes and goes, in a world without a port in which to land, without memories or nostalgia...

What if his life was a matter of simply traveling by car for a year or a millennium down roads that never ended?

Suppose he were to remain forever just two days away from his dream?

19.

The wind blew furiously.

The rain assaulted the little house. The raindrops made small designs on the wooden floor.

Juan sat up. By the light of a flash of lightning he saw the old man sleeping with his head leaning on his arm. He also discerned his fishing rod. He shook his head. His hand touched a hard case; the valise of money.

At that moment he was absolutely happy. He had found the little house again, the old man, the dunes, the sea, a terrible storm. The old man had said something to Juan that he understood quite well.

"The sea never gets seriously angry, only occasionally on the surface."

And then he explained to him that in the bottom, in the real sea, there did not exist any storms; the fish did not reel about like ships and therefore they did not experience seasickness.

Concentrate, head, remember that a short time ago you were way down by your legs... He rested the valise on his knees and touched the rolls of bills. I wonder how much there is here.

This filled him with mirth. He laughed aloud, at first as if he were being tickled in the ribs, and then louder so that he put his hand over his mouth so as not to make noise.

Something was about to happen to him. Something beautiful.

Maybe it had already happened, but his head, as usual, did not yet realize it.

His legs raised him up, his hands shut the valise that the sea had deposited on the shore and he placed it under his arm.

He pulled back the latch of the door which the wind had loosened, violently knocking down some of the tiles and the fishing rod onto the floor.

Juan secured the door from the outside with a branch. The rain made a solid wall.

The wind made his movements difficult and at times knocked him down on the wet sand. Juan would crouch down, hoping the wind would lose its strength, and then start out again. His legs carried him more steadily in spite of the storm.

"Sea, my friend, I know that you are not really mad. You are just sprinkling the empire of the earth a little."

"These legs take me straight to the great rock," he said to himself.

The rain soaked him from the outside, but happiness bathed him from within. A flash of lightning showed him the mass of rock he wanted to climb. The noise of the sea could be compared only with the flash of lightning, the thunder and the rain.

Juan reached the top, far from the reach of the foam.

"Sea, my friend," his voice was lost in the world. He shouted with all his strength.

"Sea, my friend," his voice was lost in the wind. He shouted with all his strength.

"Sea, Mr. Sea, my friend the sea..."

For a moment the clamor of the waves calmed down a bit.

"Ah, you hear me. I am your disciple," he shouted again.

He never understood very well the meaning of the word "disciple" although he knew it was a sacred word.

"I am your disciple," he repeated.

And then he threw in the valise which was lost at the bottom of the cliff.

20.

The old man's yellow buoy bobbed up and down in the water. The rod twisted violently. Don Andrés stood up and worked the fish that was pulling in all directions. At last it remained wagging its tail at the end of the line.

"A beautiful sargo," thought Juan. Immediately he felt the pull of his line. Could it be the same fish that had teased him some hours ago? This time he would allow him some tricks. The oblique light of the sun made its scales shine like silver.

"Another beautiful sargo with a flat body and small teeth in its mouth."

The old man's buoy began to bob again in the water. The fish return home at nightfall. Some large fish travel alone but the small ones travel together; thus, they defend themselves against hidden bait. They are not aware because, suddenly one of them begins to scream, jump and leap out of the water as if impelled by a piece of elastic... It takes them a while to recognize the other floating objects from the pieces of food that float about appetizingly in the half light. When the light is gone, the parents hurry to take their young, and the school of fish emigrates away from the dangerous zones.

Juan baited his line and cast the line over the perfectly green water. Perhaps the fish won't follow the movement of the sun but the color of the sea, he thought. The buoy rocked twice, then raised its head only to sink again like a squirrel.

The old man threw some stones in the water with energy to attract a greedy fish.

When the space created became full of sargos, the old man picked up his line again and wiped his hands with a rag.

"We're finished for today, boy," he smiled. "I told you we'd have a good day today, didn't I?"

Don Andrés had profound respect for the sea and its inhabitants. The beggar who becomes a miser is not a beggar. The fisherman who fishes more than he needs to is a miser.

Juan cleaned his fish hook, rolled the line around the pole, arranged the fish in the knapsack and washed his hands.

One evening, a few weeks after he had arrived, he returned indignant to the little house, because the old man had interrupted their fishing just when there were hundreds of fish available.

"Why do we wait for hours, if just when we can harvest a large number, we return?"

But today Juan returned satisfied. Fishing did not mean grabbing all the fish in the sea. The hours waiting are as rich as the hours of harvesting. The sublime art of fishing—the only way to understand the sea and to become a disciple.

That night they would eat with total tranquility. It would be a good time to ask don Andrés a few questions if sleep did not overcome him first. Reclining against the door of the little house, Juan had often fallen asleep. He would awaken the following day asleep in his bed and covered with his blanket.

21.

The two travelers were returning along the shore. They were familiar with each of the rocks along the way, the characteristics of the fisheries according to the season of the year, the tides, the color of the water and the time of day.

It was a long boat and tall. The prow buried in the sand rose four meters above the ground.

Through the years it had challenged the sea but today it only maintained an arrogant posture. The stern was set into the water with waves whirling around outside and entering with fury through the crevices. The remains of a ladder led to a small platform, a last vestige of the main deck. Juan had often climbed up the iron beams.

Don Andrés told him about the shipwreck which had occurred many years ago. A violent wind struck along the coast where there were boats of all sizes and lasted three days and three nights. The boat seemed happy to be buried near the sea. An old hulk full of dignity, with a cemetery of hundreds of kilometers all for itself.

"You say, don Andrés, that the sea is never angry; but it treated this boat very badly."

They climbed up the promontory. From there, on a stormy night, he had thrown the valise full of bills into the sea. Since that night joy was his inseparable companion. The old man never made any comments. Neither did he ask. Nevertheless, Juan knew that his gesture was decisive.

What does decisive mean? At times he surprised himself saying words whose meaning he did not really understand.

"Decisive"—"disciple..."

"Don't worry about words, boy. They can be deceiving. Instead, go find some worms because we have no bait."

After the sun sinks behind the horizon, the light remains attached to the sky for at least another hour. The sea becomes dark little by little. The dunes lose their radiant splendor, intensify their yellowishness and slowly become cold.

The pace of the two travelers quickened. Juan did not skip as he had on the trip out. The evening brought him its own tranquility.

It had been a great day for fishing. A sensational day. It was a year ago that Juan had, at that very same time, laid eyes on the little house for the first time. That had been another unforgettable journey, when the sea received him and did not allow him to die of hunger.

"Don Andrés," he said, "today it felt as if it were my birthday."

"It is your birthday, boy. I told you this morning: You're a year old and we're going to celebrate," he answered with conviction.

"I've never celebrated my birthday."

Neither did he know that day. His uncle had told him he was born on some July night.

"Today we're going to celebrate and I assure you that you're never going to forget this date. Put it into your head." The old man tapped the boy on the head with his bony knuckles.

"This morning you were right, don Andrés. Today we really made a great catch."

At a distance in the dusk was the little house. Juan ran ahead to get there first and light the lamp.

The Supper

22.

*T*hat supper was not an ordinary one. The old man took care of the most minute details. For example, he did not fry the sargos, but roasted them on the grill out of doors. He used the charcoal he kept in a bag. Juan contemplated the ceremony of the lighting of the fire until it glowed with the opaque red of the live coals. The moonless night revealed a clear sky.

He entered into the little house. The strong smell of the sea surprised him. There is nothing in the world that smells like the sea at nightfall and during the night. "It smells like life without any touch of death." Juan did not understand that saying either. For a long time there were many things he did not quite understand with his head. At least his legs took over at difficult times, when they carried him without complaining that night to the promontory on which the heavens seemed to be hurling itself down upon the earth.

Juan sat down on an old wooden crate near the door. He breathed deeply a few times. He filled himself with the sea smell: algae, sun, infinitude, wind… he was breathing life.

On the crate that served as a table, don Andrés had placed a white cloth which he got who-knows-where. The little cloth that covered the rough crate was embroidered with flowers.

Two glasses, homemade bread, a bottle of wine, and on the plates, the golden fish, warm and tender.

Juan cut it with skill, separated the spine and the vertebral column.

The old man had taught him how to eat fish without destroying it, respectfully. He took great care in teaching him and would not stand for mistakes. The sargo is a simple fish, without complications, while there are others that are very tricky with their twisted spines.

"Oh, good fish, nourish me with the strength that comes from the sea."

Juan always said a small prayer that no one had ever taught him and which he said in a loud voice. He said it for himself: a plea to the sea across the fish. About the sea of the tourists one cannot speak; but only about the sea of the little house on the dunes.

"What does our sea have that the sea of the tourists does not?"

The lamp illumined the table making the shadows long as they played against the south wall, the tiles, the fishing rods and sinkers.

Don Andrés ate slowly as if time did not count. Seated on small stools, they carried on long conversations. Juan asked all the questions and made all the comments he had formulated during the day.

Of course, there are questions one asks on clear nights, others on stormy nights, and some are reserved for the endless winter nights. That night Juan listened to the movement of the sea in the breakers, and nothing else. They ate in silence.

23.

Don Andrés changed like the sea. The intense light of the lamp illuminated one side of his bony face, his cheek slightly sunken, the prominent nose, his prominent jaw, his large ears close to his head, the fine mouth and high forehead. Hundreds of small wrinkles surrounded his eyes.

"Is it true, don Andrés, that small wrinkles come from struggling with the sunlight?"

"And when I'm old like you will my eyes be surrounded by wrinkles too?"

"My uncle has a red, round face. He drinks the wine of grapes and gets drunk." The old man had enormous eyebrows, veritable shrubs over his eyes.

"You never had much of a beard, did you?"

"No, boy, I never did."

He shaved every day with a blade he laid on a strip of leather. Andrés, with his bony dark skin, had long arms, long legs and a long body...

"How tall are you, don Andrés?"

"Don Andrés, did you ever get married?"

"Did you ever have children?"

The old man had never asked him where he came from. Nor did he know that in his neighborhood they used to call him Flea and that he was a good left-footed shooter.

Nevertheless, no one knew him better than the old man. He knew him from within. In his neighborhood of many streets and people, Juan lived lost like a leaf or an ant. In the dunes he was no longer lost like a leaf or an insect, but had been transformed into a fisherman. Perhaps even a disciple of the sea.

"Does the sea know many things, don Andrés?"

"The sea knows everything, boy."

"Even what happens on land?"

"Certainly."

"And what I am thinking?"

"What we all think."

"For the sea there are no secrets," he concluded.

He could see just one small, deep-set eye. The other remained in the shade. The long arm took the glass of wine and drew it to the mouth. The same arm cut a piece of bread which it deposited on the plate.

The scent of the sea enveloped him, possessed every pore of his skin. "The sea pauses at the shore and surrounds the earth with its aroma."

"Don Andrés, who are you?"

His voice resonated in the small house and became a part of the sea's perfume. The old man smiled. As he did so, the only eye through which he could see squinted until it was converted into a tiny point of light.

He was wrapped in a smile. Then began the tingling of laughter that spilled over from within and rose to his lips. He began to laugh.

The laughter did not stop on his lips, it reached to his eyes and ran across his forehead until his body became a vessel far too small to contain it. It advanced beyond the limits of his skin, inundated the small house and became one with the aroma from the sea.

"Tell me, little head, where does this laughter come from which is as uncontainable as the tides, impetuous as a south wind that is born on the horizon and comes during the night?"

The laughter prevented his thinking, as if everything was an affectionate joke, a game full of tenderness...

"Do you remember, don Andrés, when I threw the green bills with bag and all over the cliff?" Juan was talking in spurts, shaken as he was by his laughter.

"The wind was testing me, wasn't it?"

The lamp illuminated the old man's profile. Juan had never seen him annoyed, or scowling or ill-humored. Neither had he ever seen him as happy as that night on which they dined together.

Then the lamplight shone across the old man. Now it did not illuminate him from outside, but seemed to emanate from within: The light came from his body, from his clean and mended clothing.

Half of his body that was in the shadows became all light. Juan perceived his two small and brilliant eyes in their totality, his bony face and long arms.

His clothes became as bright as the lamplight—his trousers which came up to his calves and the shirt the old man always wore, even in the heat of summer.

The wrinkles on his skin became filled with light, his ears, the dimple in his chin, the corners of the mouth, the folds in his neck, and the cavity formed by the clavicle in men.

"The old man is a bundle of light," he said. His light illumines the little house, it extends beyond the limits of the wooden walls, plays across the beach to the west and the east passing over the cliff, dissolving the night over the sea until it reaches the horizon and proceeds toward the sky, up and up in the direction of the stars.

Never had he seen the sea so calm, nor the sand so lukewarm, nor the sky so luminous. The shadows had no place to go, everything could be seen, visible from without and from within. Things were not transparent like crystal, but luminous, consistent, solid, friendly.

The sea surrounded, penetrated and invaded everything.

The moon, the sun, the sargos, the corvines, algae, the sand on the beach, the eels, the crabs, the sensitive anemones, the octopus, the blowing of the wind, the rocks, the cliffs, men, women, yesterday, today, tomorrow. All of it remained bathed in light while Juan laughed...

His head, the weakest part of his body, was suffused with light, and he stammered:

"The old man does not come from yesterday, he is a visitor of tomorrow."

"Then, what do the wrinkles signify?"

His head became entangled again. Juan continued to repeat so as not to lose himself in the labyrinth of his thoughts.

"He comes from tomorrow, he comes from tomorrow. This sea comes from tomorrow, this earth, this light, these fishes, this sand, this aroma of life without admixture of death...

"Where does don Andrés come from?"

24.

As if the light had empowered him anew, Juan started to walk on the sand. The sea came up to the dunes, climbed the slope and washed his feet. As the sea wet them, he felt a new strength that came up to his calves. Now he did not have to push himself to conquer the inertia of the dunes.

The sea continued to rise, it reached to his knees and from his knees to his waist, soaking him from outside and inside.

"I hope it will soon reach to my head," he thought. His legs soaked with the life that came from the sea were transformed into something fantastic. He decided to visit the sea from within. He submerged himself in the sea with the speed of a buoy dragged by a large, muscular sargo. He did not feel asphyxiated, dizzy from the changes in pressure that the divers experience according to what don Andrés explained to him. The waters took him in as one of their own; the big fish embraced him with gentleness.

He was welcomed in all the schools of fish, their honored guest, the lord of their house. They showed him their caves and brought him to visit old shipwrecked ships lying there down the centuries.

They repose in peace at the bottom of the ocean, full of hope. At the surface the sea was hard on them, it gave them no quarter, nor answered their prayers, but once they penetrated its bosom he covered them with calmness and serenity.

When the plane falls from the skies, the earth rejects it and breaks it up into a thousand pieces. At times it goes up in flames becoming ashes and twisted metal. The sea, however, accepts the shipwrecked that come from other kingdoms, sustains the enormous barges and, with the delicacy of a woman, deposits them on the sandy bottom, as if it were depositing a sick person on its bed.

Once placed on the maritime floor, they become grandparents, full of noisy nieces and nephews that play in every corner of the sea floor. The algae paint them in multiple colors, the mollusks cover them anew. They surge with life.

Fishes of all shapes were playing in the mouths of large cannons, and in the holds of the ships slept the adult fishes who did not want to be disturbed by the goings and comings of the young.

Through a hole, Juan settled down in a hold. He would take a nap. He did not feel tired, but wanted to see how one slept at the bottom of the sea. He lay down. The water rocked him a moment and he fell asleep. Dreams in the sea had nothing to do with dreams on land. There was no need to close one's eyes. To sleep is to feel brother to the ships, the mollusks, the algae, the fishes, the space above the sea, the stars reflected on the surface of the water during clear nights.

The Flea, the most humble and most important of all. He was star and algae, land and space, fire and air.

Before, no one needed him. Once only was he needed by the adults to climb through a little window.

Now all needed Flea. This was a mystery his head never understood. He owed it to the old man and, above all, to the sea that received him as disciple...

Thus is the sleep at the bottom of the sea.

70

25.

The old man was eating placidly. Perhaps he was not aware that he was enveloped in light, that his wrinkles gave off a magnificent splendor, and that no part of his body remained in shadow.

Magnificent are the old man's shoulders. Broad, bony, firm. The shoulders support the weight of life, that is why they bend over when old age comes.

The Flea had always been impressed by doña Sara, all curved over like a ball of wool, a bent branch that seeks the earth. The neighbors said she was more than a hundred years old.

The Flea did not want his back to be bent over. When doña Sara died, there was a great funeral. All the neighborhood went, her children, nieces and nephews, grandchildren... It was not a sad funeral. All were speaking animatedly. Juan stood a long time by the coffin.

"Finally the years have overcome your curved back, doña Sara," he said. It had been a long struggle, one hundred years!

Something was happening that had to do with don Andrés' back, with that of doña Sara and maybe with the world's.

His laughter erupted and he couldn't stop. It was like those spurts of fresh water that appear in the sierras and prevented his drinking the wine in his glass.

"Don Andrés, your back is never going to curve over, is it?"

"No, never, boy."

"It's not like doña Sara's back, is it?"

"No."

"Is it made differently?"

"My back does not struggle with time."

"Of course," he repeated, "it doesn't struggle with time. And mine?"

"Not yet."

"Sea, my friend," he shouted.

26.

The sea wet his back in the hold of the sunken old ship. The large fish continued sleeping. The small ones peeked out from the openings and went back to take cover and continue to play with enormous chains converted into stones.

Then doña Sara appeared, rocking on her legs. She entered into the curved hold like a little woolen ball.

"Be careful, doña Sara, don't trip." Juan helped her descend the stairs.

"Doña Sara," he shouted. The old lady had gotten very deaf toward the end of her life.

The fish swam by quickly annoyed at the noise. The old lady raised her head with difficulty and looked at him with a sad expression.

The woman looked at him fixedly. Her glance was a plea.

What was the old lady asking of him?

"I'm Flea, doña Sara, a boy from the streets, poor and totally ignorant..."

72

The old lady continued to look at him with sad eyes.

"What do you want from me? Don't look at me like that!"

Then he recalled that twice the sea had not permitted him to die of hunger. Perhaps he was now its disciple and he did not realize it.

"My friend, the sea, I present you doña Sara. Look how her poor back is. Have pity. She struggled with time for a hundred years and finally lost the battle..." That was all he said.

The woman began to straighten up. Her back began to come up until it reached a vertical position. Her shoulders squared up and she could look straight ahead. Her features lost their rigidity, her eyes acquired a new brilliance and joy, her mouth became soft, her forehead serene, her legs became stable, strong, and her fingers distorted by arthritis opened up.

The small old woman attained her perfect height. The Flea saw at that moment a tall woman, elegant, robust... Her head touched the top of the hold. She came down the last steps and stood there, conqueror of time and looking at Juan as she blocked completely the opening at the entrance with her back.

Juan was shocked.

He never would have believed that this woman was doña Sara, the one who lived on the next block, around the corner from the ranch. If the neighbors saw her, they'd never recognize her. They'd say she was someone else, but it was she, it was she...

"Thank you, my friend the sea," he whispered with a calm voice.

Flea and doña Sara had always understood each other. When the old lady used to cross the street with short steps, as fragile as a piece of crystal, Flea would stop playing ball. She looked at him with affection and used to say:

"You are a good boy. Don't go with bad companions."

Now, tall, much taller than Juan, she approached him and kissed him twice on the cheeks.

"You have a powerful friend."

"I am its disciple."

Juan remained perfectly still upon hearing those words. For the first time he dared to confess he was its disciple. Its disciple forever, the fondest desire of his life had been fulfilled.

27.

Juan sipped some wine. He cut very carefully a piece of fish, while his head tried to select the words:

"Doña Sara, the real doña Sara, which one is she, don Andrés?"

"The one you have just seen at the bottom of the sea."

"I knew the other, don Andrés. She used to live around the corner from my uncle's ranch. I attended her funeral together with all the people from the neighborhood…"

"Be careful, boy, don't let yourself be deceived by your eyes: it's the future that decides the truth of things…"

He looked toward the past, he thought, toward his uncle, his neighborhood, I'm Flea. If I look ahead, I am not Flea.

"Don Andrés, who am I now?"

"A disciple."

The old man's back was magnificent, capable of carrying the world without becoming bent over. The birds have wings on their backs. The old man's back didn't need wings. Just as it was, pierced by the light, he could do anything.

"Don Andrés, I would like to have a good back like yours."

The old man bent over and extending his arm picked up his favorite fishing rod. It was long, flexible and solid. He had struggled with muscular fish down the years, many lines had been cut; but he always resisted the pull on the line. He returned immediately to his former position, straight as a cypress.

The old man took it and placed it across his knees.

Everything is perfect, said Juan to himself. Now the old man would dedicate a little time to putting his fishing gear in order. Later they would plan the next day's program. He would ask him, "Tell me, boy, where shall we go fishing tomorrow?"

And Juan would think very carefully before risking an opinion. A disciple cannot answer too hastily.

Flea was in good shape. In spite of the day's work, he felt no tiredness at all. Never in his life had he felt more agile than that night, nor been more awake.

"Don Andrés, I feel nimble and strong. Would

75

you like to go fishing during the night?" He said these words to test himself and find out if he might be dreaming.

Juan liked football. He could play for an entire day. When there was no football, he'd run around the streets. He needed to move, to run, to jump...

At that time he couldn't be still; but since he had become a disciple of the sea, he did not need to move continually. He hadn't played football for months since his arrival at the little house on the dunes, and he didn't care.

It was while he was contemplating the shining back of the old man, his mended shirt bathed in light, that Juan felt in himself a strength greater than that of sequoias. His uncle, the adults, football—all evaporated like those small puddles that the tides leave between the rocks, with the noonday sun. The sea embraced him like the air, it cut through his lungs and, passing through his blood, it ran through his body. His legs, back, arms glowed with life. He didn't need to move from the crate, or chase the ball, or climb the trees to feel his body stronger than the sequoia with a bark thousands of years old.

Until he arrived at the little house on the dunes he had been a flea that jumps up and down avoiding death.

Now he was promontory, rock, sea.

28.

The old man took his fishing knife and with great care cut the narrowest tip of his fishing pole.

He cut a piece no longer than four centimeters, that shone like his clothes, his wrinkles, his back, like the eels when they are touched by the phosphorescence of the sea.

He left the pole against the wall to concentrate on the piece selected. He polished it until he had removed all its roughness and perforated it.

Juan contemplated the old man's work. He asked himself:

"What is he doing now, cutting down his best pole, the one he never lets me use?"

From his fishing box, he chose a thin piece of leather. He tested it for its resistance and joined it to the end of the pole. A necklace of leather and a fishing pole.

"Boy," he called.

Juan came over. The old man placed around his neck the talisman he had just made with a piece of leather.

29.

"Does the sea bathe all the earth?"

"All of it."

Juan was not satisfied with the answer.

"Don Andrés, does our sea bathe all men, all animals, all the birds and stars?"

"All of them."

The wind had paused on the dunes. For the first time since coming to the house he did not hear the sound of the waves.

In the total silence he perceived a distant

melody. It could be coming from the stars, from the bottom of the sea or from the night itself. Flea had heard his uncle's radio at full volume and had learned the latest songs. The music he was hearing at this moment was not like any other, not even like the purring of the sea on tranquil nights before the storms.

Maybe what he was hearing was not music, but something different which he in his ignorance called music. Maybe it was wind which, when it arrived, would change the shape of the dunes into some other geometric designs.

In any case, the music or the wind was entering his ears (of that he had no doubt), invaded his head and from there ran through his body. Later the music left him and continued on its way.

Juan sang drawn by the music that reached him. His well-tuned voice flowed from within him without effort, without previous training, just as laughter had spilled out, and joined the great concert.

The music passed over him like those bands of wild ducks that he so often watched navigating through the heavens. Juan felt their call and joined the migratory birds in the march toward the unknown.

His song, like the light, made him a brother to the trees, the sargo, the sea-gull, the mollusks, the wild flowers that spring up in the sand.

"This melody is the murmur of the sea that covers all men." His head did not understand the phrase.

"Tell me, don Andrés, who am I? What is my name?"

This question formed part of the song, of the light, of the salty smell, of the total calm.

30.

Juan found himself at the bottom of the sea, in a section of a sunken vessel, in the midst of a limitless valley.

"The bottom of this sea knows no limits," he said. "I could spend all my life looking and I would always see more."

Perhaps that was a characteristic of the sea from within. Nevertheless, the old man had explained something else to him:

"The divers, boy, see less than we do. The water does not have the transparence of the air."

For once don Andrés had been mistaken all around; although it is certain that the divers need heavy equipment so as not to drown, he was very comfortable without a diver's suit.

Through the limitless valley swam fishes of all sizes and shapes, tortoises with huge shells, catfish that shrink and stretch to swim, eels, seals, sea-wolfs...All the forms he had drawn upon the sand near the shack, and countless more plants, algae, flowers...

The music continued to sound together with the light.

He raised his eyes and saw a charred forest hundreds of kilometers in size, sunken like a ship's hulk, its trunks blackened, cracked, fallen upon an earth that was an ashen color.

"Poor forest," he thought, "maybe someone built a fire one night to keep warm, did not watch it carefully and the flames destroyed the trees that cannot flee from danger."

He descended without haste, gently, until he touched the sand at the bottom of the sea. There the trees were straight, they had strong roots, had branches, leaves, flowers and fruit. They were luxuriant, young, flexible. The soil lost its ashen color and was covered with plants that climbed up the trunks.

The music that was coming nearer became more intense.

"Now the fire will never destroy the forests. They are new forests like doña Sara's back, forests that do not struggle with time."

Juan contemplated the bottom of the sea that was now a forest. Then, as if emerging from the trees, appeared animals of all sizes and birds with brilliant plumage. The animals strolled through the forest. The fish greeted them like one receives long-awaited guests.

"Now there exists but one kingdom," thought Juan.

He again raised his eyes and saw falling down men, women, children, mutilated, paralytic, beaten, burned, covered with wounds, malnourished, dead... They were falling slowly, like the charred trunks, and they touched the sand and their bodies were re-created. With those remains another humanity was formed.

Thus did the sea fill up with men, women, animals, cities, forests. All falling like drops of a torrential rainfall, and populating the ocean.

31.

When he opened his eyes, the sun was beginning to rise. The light was filtering through the slits in the walls of the little house.

Flea, seated on his crate, listened to the clash of the sea against the coastline. A ray of sunshine fell upon the fishing poles.

"Don Andrés," he called.

Juan knew it was useless to call him. The old man had disappeared like the light, in total silence.

He stood up and stretched. He opened the door of the small house to contemplate the dunes and the morning sea which is always bluish.

"Good morning, my friend the sea."

He closed the door of the shack behind him.

"Good-bye, little house on the dunes, full of the scent of the sea, my only home." His head, as usual, did not understand what he was doing; but his legs had a firm and clear purpose.

He began to sink himself in the dunes. His lips parted and, for the first time, he hummed the new music that was wind and order, the same melody that the old man used to whistle among the breakers on fishing days.

"You are headed for the station," guessed his head.

He descended an enormous dune and lost the view of the sea.

"I am a disciple of the sea," he shouted.

Barefoot, because he had forgotten his sandals at the house, his trousers and mended shirt, Juan the Flea.

He brought his hand up to his chest: he touched the necklace with the piece of leather the old man had cut, felt the thrill of happiness that was present with the melody his lips were whistling.

Then his feet began to run, leaving small footprints on the damp sand of early morning.